this book belongs to

....

love Little M x

otter 🐾

Prince Marino

Thanks, kittie,
love Snow & Jack xx

For K&E – A.L.
For Sarah – L.B.

THE FAIRYTALE HAIRDRESSER AND THE SUGAR PLUM FAIRY
A PICTURE CORGI BOOK 978 0 552 57272 9
Published in Great Britain by Picture Corgi, an imprint of Random House
Children's Publishers UK. A Penguin Random House Company

Penguin
Random House
UK

This edition published 2015
1 3 5 7 9 10 8 6 4 2

Text copyright © Abie Longstaff, 2015
Illustrations copyright © Lauren Beard, 2015
The right of Abie Longstaff and Lauren Beard to be identified as the author
and illustrator of this work has been asserted in accordance with the
Copyright, Designs and Patents Act 1988. All rights reserved.
No part of this publication may be reproduced, stored in a retrieval system,
or transmitted in any form or by any means, electronic, mechanical,
photocopying, recording or otherwise, without the prior permission of
the publishers. Picture Corgi Books are published by Random House
Children's Publishers UK, 61–63 Uxbridge Road, London W5 5SA

www.randomhousechildrens.co.uk
www.randomhouse.co.uk

Addresses for companies within The Random House Group
Limited can be found at: www.randomhouse.co.uk/offices.htm
THE RANDOM HOUSE GROUP
Limited Reg. No. 954009
A CIP catalogue record for this book is
available from the British Library.
Printed in China

Penguin Random House is committed to a sustainable future
for our business, our readers and our planet. This book is
made from Forest Stewardship Council® certified paper.

The Fairytale Hairdresser

and the

SUGAR PLUM FAIRY

PICTURE CORGI

Abie Longstaff & Lauren Beard

Kittie Lacey was the best hairdresser in all the land.

On the day of the Winter Ballet, Kittie's salon was the busiest place in town. Everyone in Fairyland Village wanted to look their best for the show.

Kittie was very excited! She would be dancing with her ballerina friend, Clara. But first she had a lot of work to do.

The seven fairies asked for extra sparkles on their wings.

Rapunzel needed an enormous ballet bun.

And Prince Florian and Princess Rose wanted matching ribbons on their ballet slippers.

When Clara arrived she was covered in snow.

"It's so good to see you!" Kittie said, giving her friend a hug. "Let's go and decorate the tree – I have some sparkly ribbon that will be perfect."

Clara had brought a beautiful wooden nutcracker for the tree,
carved in the shape of a little soldier.

"My uncle found him in the woods yesterday and gave him to me,"
she said, as they walked through the snow. "He's lovely!"

The enormous tree by the ballet theatre looked beautiful.
Everyone had put something on the branches to decorate it for
the show. Kittie reached up and added her sparkly red ribbon
and Clara placed her nutcracker right in the middle.

But Kittie noticed someone was upset!
It was the Sugar Plum Fairy.
"What's wrong?" asked Kittie.

"Prince Armand is missing!" the Sugar
Plum Fairy sobbed. "Everyone in the
Land of Sweets is looking for him. We're
putting up posters all over Fairyland."

MISSING

HAVE YOU SEEN THIS PRINCE?

LOOK OUT!

MICE ABOUT

If you see them call the pied piper hotline

BISCUITS FIT FOR ROYAL TEA

"Ohhh!" sobbed the fairy. "I hope that evil Mouse King and Queen haven't hurt him!"

Kittie gave her a hug. "Don't worry, love. We'll find the Prince."

"We'll help you search the Land of Sweets," said Rose.

"Oh, thank you!" said the Sugar Plum Fairy. She waved her wand and . . .

. . . to their amazement, the friends shrank

down,

down,

down . . .

. . . until they were no bigger than the sweets and toys on the tree!

The fairy parted the branches of the
enormous tree to reveal a hidden kingdom.
"Welcome to the Land of Sweets!" she cried.

WELCOME
TO THE Magical LAND
OF SWEETS

Kittie had never been to the Land of Sweets before. She followed the Sugar Plum Fairy down a jellybean path, past gingerbread houses and liquorice lampposts. "It's so beautiful here," she sighed.

"I could stay for ever!" agreed Clara, gazing at the little sugar flowers.
"Although we DO need to get back for the Winter Ballet."
They hunted high and low for Prince Armand, but he was nowhere to be found.

Suddenly there was a cry from the Candy Cane Tower. "Watch out! The mice are coming!"

"Those naughty mice are always trying to eat our houses," the Sugar Plum Fairy told Kittie. "Without the Prince to stop them, we'll need all the help we can get!"

She waved her wand, and by magic . . .

. . . all the toys on the Christmas tree came to life!

Clara's nutcracker instantly took charge. The toys fought bravely to defend the Land of Sweets against the evil Mouse King and Queen.

The slinkies
blocked the path.

The jack-in-the-box
popped up to scare
the mice away.

And the teddy bears
held off the attackers.

The Mouse King and Queen were furious.
"Bite the nutcracker!" they cried, charging towards Clara's beloved toy.
"Nooo!" shouted Clara. "Kittie! Help!"

Kittie looked around her – there on the branches was her sparkly red ribbon.

The ribbon seemed enormous now!
Kittie pulled one end of the fabric towards her.
"Take the other end!" she called to Clara.

Kittie and Clara danced round and round the Mouse King and Queen,
wrapping the ribbon tight. In moments the mice were trapped!

"Hooray for Kittie and Clara!" cried the Sugar Plum Fairy, as the Mouse King and Queen were marched off to prison. Clara threw her arms around the nutcracker.

"I'm so glad you're safe!" she said, and she kissed him.

To Clara's amazement the nutcracker jumped and shook.
Then, in a swirl of magic . . .

. . . he turned into a handsome prince!
"Prince Armand!" cried the Sugar Plum Fairy.

"Yes, it's me," said the Prince. "The Mouse King turned me into a nutcracker. But you saved me!" He gazed into Clara's eyes. "I couldn't let those mice hurt you," said Clara, gazing right back.

"Clara," – the Prince bent down on one knee – "please will you stay with me in the Land of Sweets?" "I will!" said Clara and everybody cheered.

The Sugar Plum Fairy clapped her hands. "Let's celebrate!"
"Come and dance with us in the ballet tonight!" said Kittie.
"I'd love to," said the fairy, "but I don't have anything special to wear."
Kittie smiled. "I think I can help with that," she said.

Kittie found the perfect
outfit for the Sugar Plum Fairy
just in time for the show.

"Quick!" said Kittie. "Take us
back to Fairyland Village!"

The Sugar Plum Fairy waved her wand and Kittie and her
friends grew up, **up**, **up** until they were normal size again.
Everyone took their place . . .

. . . and Fairyland danced the night away
at the best Winter Ballet ever!
The Sugar Plum Fairy was the star of the show!

And, from that day on, whenever
her little friends needed a makeover,
Kittie made the magic trip to the
Land of Sweets.